★ JULIA DONALDSON ★

Princess Mirror-Belle

and the Magic Shoes

Turn the page to read an extract . . .

Illustrated by
✳ LYDIA MONKS ✳

Chapter One

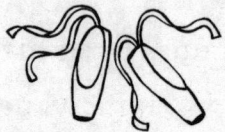

The Magic Shoes

"Hey, you! Yes, you! Turn around, look over your shoulder," sang Ellen's brother, Luke, into the microphone.

Ellen was sitting in the village hall watching Luke's band, Breakneck, rehearse for the Battle of the Bands. The hall was nearly empty, but that evening it would be packed with fans of the six different bands who were entering the competition.

As well as being Breakneck's singer,

Luke wrote most of their songs, including this one.

"It's me! Yes, me! Turn around, I'm still here," he sang. Then he wandered moodily around the stage, while the lead guitarist, Steph, played a twangy solo.

Steph, who never smiled, wore frayed baggy black trousers with a pointless chain hanging out of the pocket and a black T-shirt with orange flames on it. The solo went on and on.

"Steph's so good at the guitar," Ellen whispered to Steph's sister Seraphina, who was sitting next to her.

"I know," said Seraphina. She was two years older than Ellen and dressed very much like her brother, except that her T-shirt had a silver skull on it. "But I bet they don't win. I don't think they should have chosen this song. It's not going to get people dancing. Steph wrote a much better one called 'Savage'."

Ellen couldn't imagine Steph writing anything dancy, but she was quite shy of Seraphina and didn't say so. Besides, she had just remembered something.

"Dancing – help! I'm going to be late for ballet!" She picked up a bag from the floor.

"You've got the wrong bag – that's mine," said Seraphina, who also went to ballet, but to a later class.

"Sorry." Ellen grabbed her own bag and hurried to the door.

At least she didn't have far to go. The ballet classes were held in a room called

the studio, which was above the hall. Ellen
ran up the stairs.

The changing room was empty. The
other girls must be in the studio already,
but Ellen couldn't hear any music so the
class couldn't have started yet.

Hurriedly, she put on her leotard and

ballet shoes and scooped her hair into the hairnet that Madame Jolie, the ballet teacher, insisted they all wear. Madame Jolie was very fussy about how they looked and could pounce on a girl for the smallest thing, such as crossing the ribbons on her ballet shoes in the wrong way.

Ellen was just giving herself a quick check in the full-length mirror when a voice said, "What's happened to your feet?"

It was a voice that she knew very well. It was coming from the mirror and it belonged to Princess Mirror-Belle.

About the Author and Illustrator

Julia Donaldson is one of the UK's most popular children's writers. Her award-winning books include *What the Ladybird Heard, The Snail and the Whale* and *The Gruffalo*. She has also written many children's plays and songs, and her sell-out shows based on her books and songs are a huge success. She was the Children's Laureate from 2011 to 2013, campaigning for libraries and for deaf children, and creating a website for teachers called picturebookplays.co.uk. Julia and her husband Malcolm divide their time between Sussex and Edinburgh. You can find out more about Julia at www.juliadonaldson.co.uk.

Lydia Monks studied Illustration at Kingston University, graduating in 1994 with a first-class degree. She is a former winner of the Smarties Bronze Award for *I Wish I Were a Dog* and has illustrated many books by Julia Donaldson. Her illustrations have been widely admired.

Also available

For younger readers